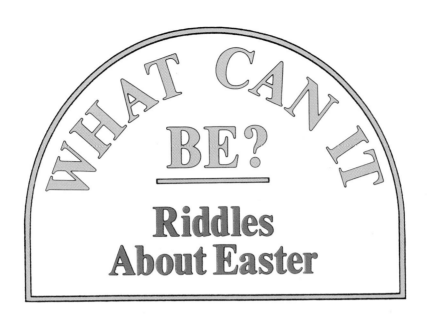

WHAT CAN IT BE?

Riddles About Easter

By Jill Ashley

Original Photography by Rob Gray

Silver Press

Published by Silver Press, a division of
Silver Burdett Press, Inc.
Simon & Schuster, Inc.
Prentice Hall Bldg., Englewood Cliffs, NJ 07632.

Printed in the United States of America.

Library of Congress Cataloging-in-Publication Data

Ball, Jacqueline A.,
Riddles about Easter / by Jackie Ball; photographs by Rob Gray.
p.   cm.   (What can it be?)
Summary: A collection of rhyming riddles describing various aspects of Easter and its celebration.

1. Riddles, Juvenile.   2. Easter——Juvenile poetry.
[1. Easter.   2. Riddles.]   I. Gray, Rob, 1952- ill.   II. Title.
III. Series.
PN6371.5.B235   1991   818′ .5402——dc20

ISBN 0–671–72726–5 (lib. bdg.)   90–8981
ISBN 0–671–72727–3   CIP
                                                  AC

WHAT CAN IT BE? concept created by Jacqueline A. Ball
Thomas Goddard/Goddard Design, Design Consultant
Photograph of choir © 1990 Allen Russell/Profiles West
Thanks to: The Ukrainian Museum, Cathedral of St. John the Divine

Within my walls,
so many pray
on Easter. . .
such a holy day.
Inside are pews;
on top, a steeple.
My bells ring out
to call the people.

What am I?

CHURCH

Easter is the most important Christian holiday of the year. Christians believe Jesus Christ was the son of God. Jesus was nailed to a cross, or crucified. Christians go to church on Easter to celebrate the Resurrection of Jesus Christ. Resurrection means "rising again." Christians believe Jesus rose, or came back to life, three days after dying on the cross.

A beautiful picture
that's not made of paints,
I tell holy stories
of Christ and the saints.
I'm built of fine pieces
of sparkling glass.
I color the sunbeams
as through me they pass.

What am I?

A STAINED GLASS WINDOW

Stained glass windows in a church show holy scenes from the life of Jesus and the saints. The saints were holy people who devoted their lives to Jesus. Church windows often show pictures that tell the story of Easter.

Our flowers bloom
in snowy white.
We're certainly a pretty sight.
At church or home,
we smell just great.
On Easter we help celebrate.

What are we?

EASTER LILIES

The pure white flowers of Easter lilies stand for new life and the Resurrection. Since Jesus came back to life, Easter celebrates the idea of life after death. White lilies decorate church altars all over the world on Easter Sunday.

Some keep their voices
so low when they sing.
But that's not what we do.
It's just not our thing.
We stand all together.
We wait for a chord.
Then we sing loud praises
of joy to the Lord.

What are we?

A CHURCH CHOIR

On Easter Sunday church choirs sing some of the most beautiful, joyful church music. The highest voices in a choir are the sopranos. The lowest are the basses. Altos and tenors are in between.

I'm soft and I'm fleecy.
You may hear me bleat.
Without me the springtime
would not be complete.
My mom is a ewe.
My dad is a ram.
So what does that make me?
A woolly white ____.

LAMB

A lamb is a baby sheep. People think of a new-born lamb as being innocent. Long ago, people sometimes killed lambs as offerings to God. Jesus is called "the lamb of God." This is because He was killed even though He was innocent. Christians believe He died for the sins of others. Forty days after Easter, Christians celebrate Ascension. This is when Jesus was taken into heaven.

Not winter, not summer,
I'm right in between. . .
the season when treetops
turn lacy and green.
A time when the clouds burst
with warm, breezy showers,
I bring perfect weather
for robins and flowers.

What am I?

SPRING

Easter comes each spring when the earth begins to bloom with new life. Spring, which comes after gloomy winter, is the perfect season for Easter. The holiday reminds Christians of Christ's Resurrection, or new life after death. Easter may fall on a Sunday, any time from March 22 to April 25.

With big, long ears that flip and flop,
I welcome everyone.
I pass out eggs and jellybeans.
I'm part of Easter fun.
I jump and hop from place to place.
I'm part of all the action.
With all I do at Easter time,
I'm such a big attraction!

What am I?

THE EASTER BUNNY

Long ago in Germany people told stories about an Easter hare. Today the Easter bunny, or rabbit, is popular. Rabbits have many babies that remind people of the beginning of spring and new life.

Soft and fluffy,
pale yellow,
I'm a tired little fellow.
Pecking through
a shell so thick
is such hard work for me, a ____.

CHICK

Chicks and many other baby animals are often born in the spring. Like bunnies and eggs, chicks are symbols of new life. They remind Christians of the rising of Jesus Christ on Easter Sunday.

Take your place.
Then say grace.
Eat some ham.
Taste the lamb.
Pass the peas.
Salad, please.
Try the pie.
Don't be shy.
I'm a meal,
so ideal.
Fill your plate.
Celebrate.

What am I?

EASTER DINNER

The forty days before Easter are called Lent. During that time Christians often give up many of their favorite foods, such as sweets. This is to show they are sorry for their sins, or things they may have done wrong. Easter Sunday marks the end of Lent. It is a time to celebrate and eat foods that were given up for Lent. Many families get together to share Easter dinner together.

Chocolate bunnies,
jellybeans,
sugar chicks,
grass so green.
Candy lambs,
lollipops,
minty eggs,
gummy drops.
I hold sweets
like these and more. . .
Easter goodies
you adore.

What am I?

AN EASTER BASKET

Many Christians give and receive baskets filled with sweet treats on Easter. The custom may have started in Germany. The German Easter hare carried red, blue, and green eggs in its Easter basket.

We started life in simple style.
Our mother was a hen.
But we weren't meant to stay that way.
Just look at us again.
Yes, once our shells were plain and white.
Our yolks were soft and runny.
But look! We're firm and fancy now,
and carried by a bunny!

Who are we?

EASTER EGGS

The Easter bunny carries eggs in its baskets. Eggs remind Christians of new life and the Resurrection. The world's fanciest Easter eggs are called *pysanky*. They are made in Russia and Poland. In Greece, children hit eggs together. They say, "Christ is risen. Truly Christ is risen." Each one tries to be the last one with an unbroken eggshell.

Mix milk and flour with some yeast.
So perfect for an Easter feast!
Add sugar, eggs, and butter too.
Then bake me golden. . .
through and through.
With eggs inside,
hard-cooked and dyed
a brilliant shade of red,
I'm such a special braided treat.
I'm sweet Greek Easter _____.

BREAD

Greek Easter bread is called *tsoureki*. It is often sweetened with orange juice, sugar, and almonds. Tsoureki is usually braided and decorated with red eggs. Bakers often use left-over bread dough to make special treats. They shape this dough into tiny baskets or animals that they give to children.

I'm a splendid treasure hunt. . .
a game of hide and seek.
You search around
the grass and ground,
on rocks and in the creek.
You look for eggs or jellybeans,
and other festive sweets.
I'm so much fun, so please join in.
I'm one of Easter's treats.

What am I?

AN EASTER EGG HUNT

Easter egg hunts and Easter egg rolls are popular in many countries. Since 1878, children have been invited to the White House in Washington, D.C. to roll Easter eggs.

We may have pretty pictures
in colors soft and bold.
We may have funny poems,
or prayers touched with gold.
We're filled with warmest wishes,
for one bright holiday.
You sign us on the bottom,
then send us on our way.

What are we?

EASTER CARDS

People in many countries enjoy sending and receiving greeting cards on Easter. In Sweden, people tell stories about witches who fly away to meet the devil at Easter time. Because of the story, Swedish children send letters with drawings of witches instead of bunnies.

Dressed-up people looking fine.
Big ones, small ones in a line.
There's a hat with feathers on it.
What a fancy Easter bonnet!
Every suit and every shoe,
every topcoat looks brand-new.
You look great. Don't be afraid. . .
to stroll right in the Easter _____.

PARADE

Strolling through the streets in fine, new Easter clothes is a tradition in many European towns. In New York City, there is a big Easter parade every year. People put on new spring clothes and fancy hats, and walk on Fifth Avenue after church services on Easter Sunday.